Silly Old Pirates Are Lost

by Jay Dale
illustrated by Alessandro Valdrighi

London Borough of Merton

M00748933

"Get up! Get up!"
shouted the captain.
"I want to go to Treasure Chest Island.
I want to find treasure!"

3

"Yes, Captain!"

said the two silly old pirates.

"But do we go left?

Or do we go right?"

"Take this map," said the captain.

"And find out.

I'm going to take my morning nap."

The big pirate with the little hat looked at the little pirate with the big hat.

"Can you read a map?" asked the big pirate.

"No," said the little pirate.
"But I can try!"

So off they went over the blue sea.
The ship went up and down.

"Look!" shouted the little pirate.
"I can see Big Hills Island."

"Yes!" said the big pirate.
"And there is Little Hills Island."

"So Treasure Chest Island
is over there,"
said the little pirate.

"Yes!" smiled the big pirate.
"That **has** to be
Treasure Chest Island."

9

"Captain! Captain!"
shouted the little pirate.
"Get up!"

The captain came up the steps.
He looked cross.
"You woke me up," he said.

"Look over there!"

shouted the two silly old pirates.

"It's Treasure Chest Island!"

The captain was very quick.

He got into the little boat.

"I will take all the treasure," he laughed.

"It will **all** be for me!

Ha! Ha! Ha!"

And off he went.

The two silly old pirates looked out.

They saw a sign.

It said, CROCODILE ISLAND.

"Oh, dear," said the silly old pirates.
"We got lost!"